Snowballs

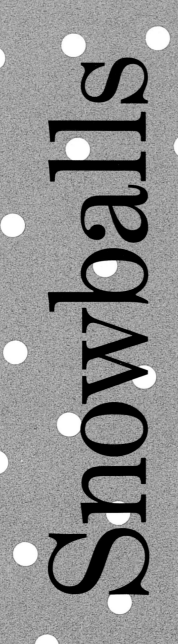

Voyager Books
Harcourt Brace & Company
San Diego   New York   London

Snowballs
Lois Ehlert

Requests for permission to make copies of any part of
the work should be mailed to: Permissions Department,
Harcourt Brace & Company, 6277 Sea Harbor Drive,
Orlando, Florida 32887-6777.

First Voyager Books edition 1999
Voyager Books is a registered trademark of
Harcourt Brace & Company.

The Library of Congress has cataloged the hardcover
edition as follows:

Ehlert, Lois.
Snowballs/Lois Ehlert.—1st ed.
p. cm.
Summary: Some children create a family out of snow.
Includes labeled pictures of all the items they use, as well
as information about how snow is formed.
ISBN 0-15-200747-7
ISBN 0-15-202095-0 pb
[1. Snow—Fiction.] 1. Title.
PZ7.E3225Sn 1995
[E]—dc20   94-47183

F E D C B

Printed in Singapore

Do you think birds know when it's going to snow?

I do. The seeds we left out were almost gone.

New Snow would soon bury the rest.

We'd been waiting for a really big snow, saving good stuff in a sack. Finally it was a perfect snowball day.

We rolled
three snowballs
and made a
snow dad.

Added a
snow mom

and
a cool
snow
boy.

Made a snow girl!

Built our cat and to end the day,

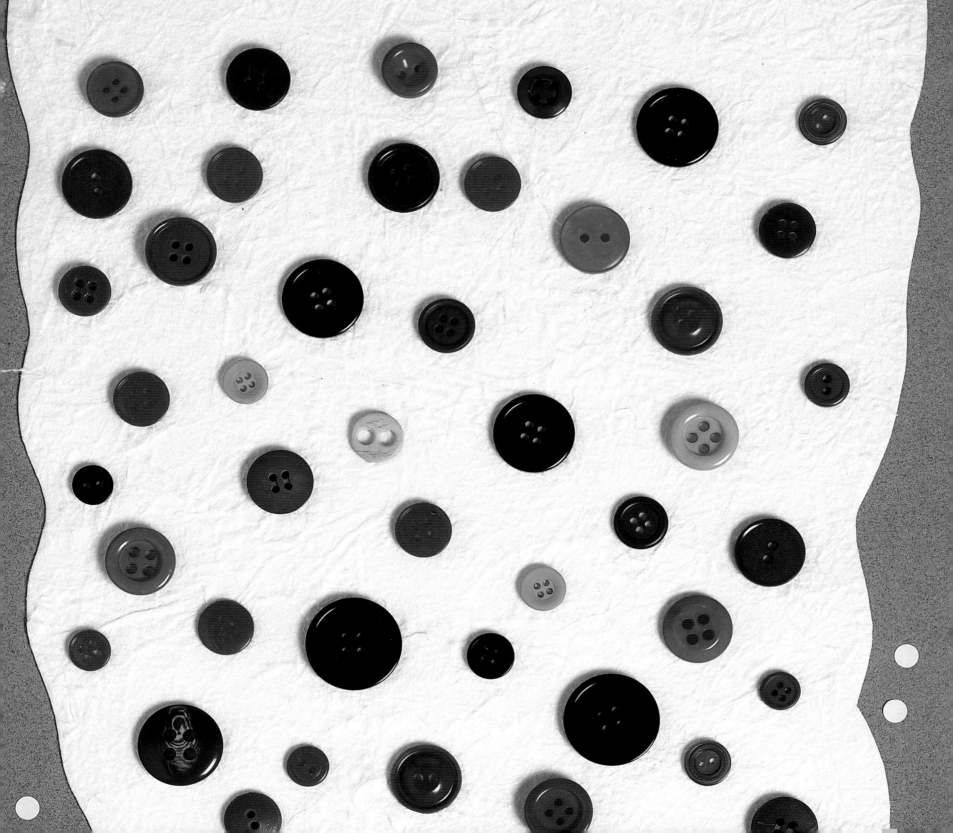

made our dog, Spot.

I guess you know what happened when the sun came out.

Snow dad's shrinking.

Mom is mush.
Boy's a blob;
girl is slush.

Baby's melting;
cat's getting small.
Dog is a puddle.

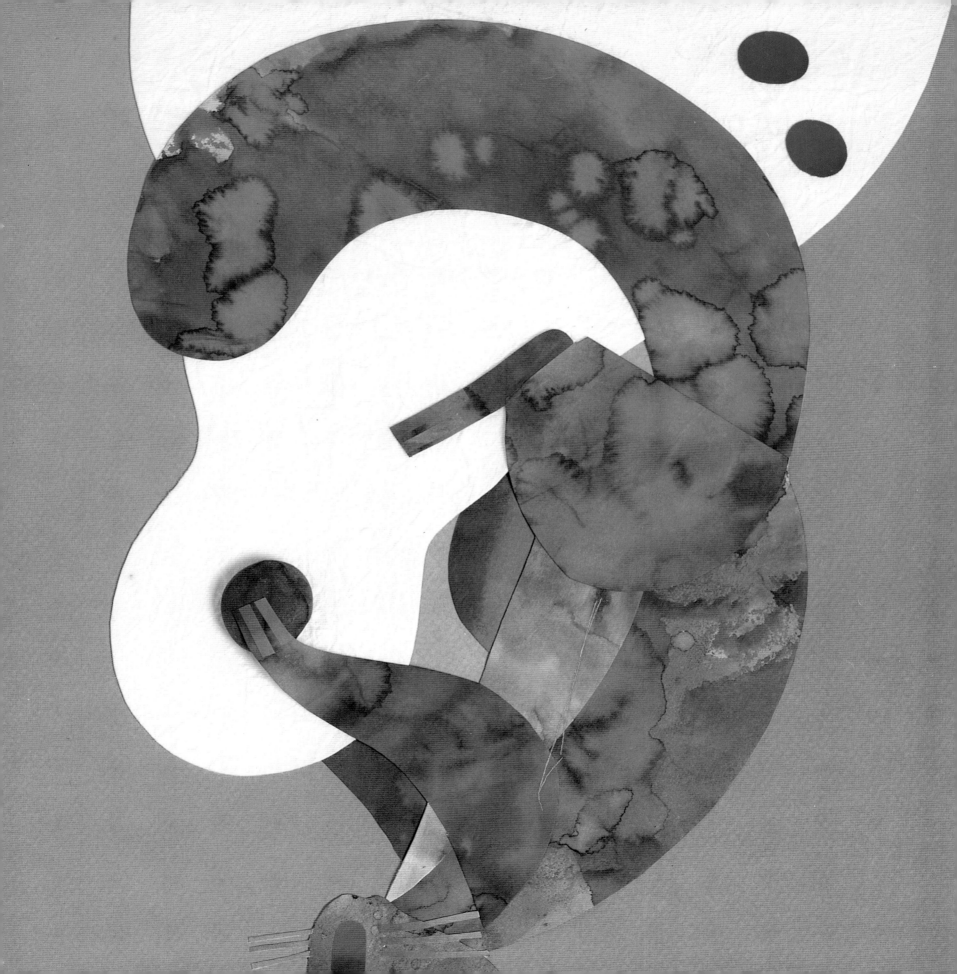

So long,
snowball.

good stuff

pine cone

toy fish

pencil

cinnamon stick

metal washer

pressed maple leaf

toy wheel

seashell

claim check

CLAIM CHECK
See Reverse Side
for Conditions
34-080

Japanese stone

twig

Mexican scrub brush

button

Thai appliqué heart

evergreen branch

bottle cap

walnut

foil candy wrapper

corn

fork

Guatemalan belt and tie

What makes it snow?

Although we can't always see the process, water is constantly evaporating from earth, changing from its liquid form to water vapor, its gas form. If you boil water, steam rises as gas. If your windows are cold, steam collects on the glass, cools, turns back into liquid, and water droplets run down your windows.

Imagine this process happening on a much larger scale. Water from our oceans, lakes, streams, and rivers evaporates, or turns into water vapor, which goes into the atmosphere. The water vapor blows around in the wind, clings to bits of dust and salt in the air, and gradually forms a cloud.

When a cloud becomes saturated with water vapor, it releases the droplets and water returns to earth. The temperature in the cloud determines whether it will release rain, snow, or other forms of precipitation, such as hail and sleet. If the cloud is warm, it will rain. If the temperature in the cloud is cold enough, water droplets freeze into ice crystals and snowflakes will fall. If the air below the cloud is warm, the snowflakes melt and fall as rain. If the air below is cool, the snow will continue its journey to earth.

If the earth is warm, snow melts when it lands. If it's cold, snow covers the ground, and that could mean a snowball day—at least until the warm sun comes out and melts the snow. Then the process of evaporation begins all over again.

Photographs are by Lillian Schultz except the three at the far right of this page, which are by Richard Ehlert, and the ones at the top and bottom left of this page, which are by Allyn Johnston.

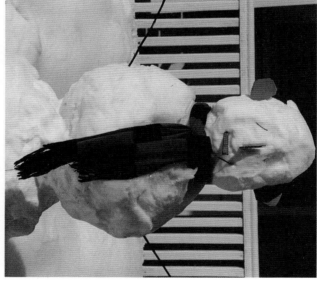

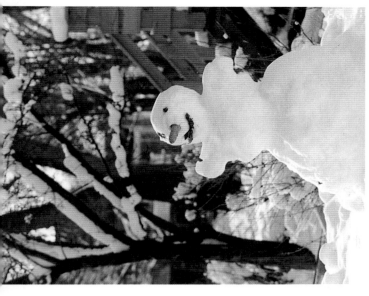
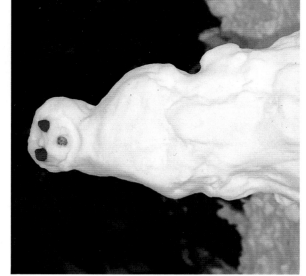

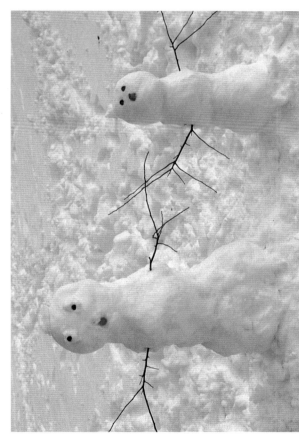

Afghani glove

Wisconsin mitten

What is snow?

Snow is a frozen, solid form of water. Water can take three forms:

gas—droplets dispersed in air, such as steam or fog

liquid—rain, oceans, lakes, streams, rivers, and drinking water

solid—ice, snowflakes, hail, sleet, and frost

clothespin

clothesline

Italian mitten

Korean glove

Wisconsin mitten

snow info

Guatemalan purse

luggage tag

MKE
MILWAUKEE
Wisconsin

Bolivian hat

crayon

Made in U.S.A. RED

NONTOXIC

peanut

strawberry

cranberry

African
kente cloth

screw

English
silk tie

Peruvian sock

telephone wire

sunflower
seeds

metal nut

jingle
bell

coffee
bean

raisin

twine

ribbon

popcorn

toy compass